"What's happening, Tommy?" Chuckie wailed.

"I think we're taking off!" Tommy shouted above the noise of the engine.

Dactar shuddered and groaned. The flying machine seemed to tilt and spin. The babies grabbed on to each other.

For a second, it felt like the Dactar flying machine was falling, but before anyone could get too scared, the machine landed with a loud CRUNCH! and a THUMP!

When the smoke cleared, they were safely on the ground. Everyone tumbled out of the machine. As Angelica and Tommy took Dil and his baby seat out, Dactar was still talking.

"*Benvenuti in Italiaaaaa.* Wellllcommme to IIIItaaaalllyyyy . . ." The voice slowed down before coming to a final stop.

The Rugrats Files

A Time Travel Adventure Series

#1 Case of the Missing Gold

#2 Yo Ho Ho and a Bottle of Milk

#3 The Quest for the Holey Pail

#4 Tale of the Unfinished Masterpiece

THE Rugrats™ FiLES

A TiME TRAVEL ADVENTURE

TALE OF THE UNFiNiSHED MASTERPiECE

Based on the TV series *Rugrats*® created by Arlene Klasky, Gabor Csupo, and Paul Germain as seen on Nickelodeon®.

ISBN 0-439-29115-1

12 11 10 9 8 7 6 5 4 3 2 1   1 2 3 4 5 6/0

Printed in the U.S.A.

First Scholastic printing, May 2001

A TIME TRAVEL ADVENTURE

TALE of the UNFINISHED MASTERPIECE

by Maria Rosado

SCHOLASTIC INC.
New York Toronto London Auckland Sydney
Mexico City New Delhi Hong Kong

CHAPTER 1

"Clear the decks, everybody!" Stu Pickles called across the backyard. "I'm starting the countdown. Then it's up, up, and away!"

Tommy looked up from the game of toss-the-teddy he was playing with his friends Chuckie, Phil, Lil, and Kimi.

"Not again!" Lil groaned.

"Do we hafta?" Phil sighed.

But Tommy's new grandma, Lulu, cheerfully leaped up from her lounge chair. She scooped up the babies and, in a moment, had them all safely stashed in the playpen on the other side of the yard. Lulu even propped an umbrella on top of the playpen as an extra precaution. "Ready when you are, Stu!" she called merrily.

Stu picked up a small remote control. He touched a big red button and started counting down, "Ten . . . nine . . ."

Of course, the last fifteen times Stu finished his countdown, the Dactar flying machine hadn't moved an inch. But you never knew what might happen when Stu tested his latest invention.

"Two . . . one!" Stu banged on the red button. "Dactar is blasting off!"

A puff of smoke snorted out the back of the flying machine. The big pterodactyl-like craft whirred and groaned.

"Go, Dactar!" the babies cheered from underneath the umbrella. For a second it looked like the dinosaur might actually lift off. Then Dactar gave a loud groan— *uurrrgggh*—and its wings drooped back down. The engine sputtered to a stop.

"Now what?" Stu poked the red button

again and again. Nothing happened, not even a puff of smoke.

"You can hit that button from now till next Tuesday and it won't do you any good," said Grandpa Lou. "That fancy contraption will never take off with all those thinggummies you got on there."

Stu patted the side of his flying machine fondly. He'd been tinkering with it for weeks, trying to switch it from pedal-power to engine-power. "But I had to add a cabin, Pop, so the whole family could use it. And a CD player. . . ."

Stu sighed. "Not to mention the ultra-deluxe detachable baby seat. Dactar has to compete with all those minivans out there."

"Maybe, but nobody expects them to fly," Lou pointed out.

"Don't you listen to him," Lulu told Stu. She unlocked the playpen so the babies could crawl out. "I'm sure Dactar will be flying in a jiffy."

Stu nodded and pulled out a screwdriver. He tightened a bolt in the CD player and one in the engine. "Maybe I should take another look at those gears, too."

"I didn't know Dactar had ears," Chuckie told Tommy as the babies toddled across the grass.

"A'course he does," Tommy said. "How else could Dactar hear my daddy count?"

"Do you think your daddy will ever make Dactar fly?" asked Lil.

"Sure!" Tommy said. "He's smarter than anybody."

"But Dactar's not flying now . . . ," Kimi observed. Then she picked up Tommy's teddy bear, wound up like a baseball pitcher, and let loose with her best throw. "Let's play toss-the-teddy some more!"

Phil and Lil both ran after the flying bear but bumped into each other and tumbled over, giggling.

"I got it! I got it!" Chuckie yelled,

running with his hands outstretched.

"No, I got it!" Angelica suddenly appeared from around the corner of the house. She snatched the bear out of the air, just inches above Chuckie's fingers.

"Hi, Angelica," Tommy said. "Wanna play toss-the-teddy with us?"

Angelica snorted, dangling the teddy bear out of Chuckie's reach. "Why would I want to play with a bunch of baldy babies?"

"'Cause it's fun?" Kimi suggested.

Angelica ignored her. "I can't play with you babies, anyways, even if I wanted to . . . which I don't," Angelica said, "because I gots a boo-boo. See?" She showed off a tiny bandage on her knee. "My daddy took me to the doctor to fix it."

Kimi sniffed. "I don't go to the doctor for a boo-boo. My mommy just kisses it to make it better."

Angelica made a face at Kimi. "What do

you know? See, when you goes to the doctor for a boo-boo, he gives you lollipopses to make you stop cryin'. And my daddy gives me pennies and nickels and dimes," she added, showing off a handful of change.

"A'course I was only pretending to cry," Angelica announced proudly. "The doctor had to give me six-gazillion lollipopses before I stopped."

Kimi didn't care about Angelica's boo-boo or lollipops. She reached for the teddy, but Angelica was too quick. She tossed the teddy bear into the playpen.

"If you don't wanna play with us, why'd you come?" Kimi asked, frowning.

Angelica just rolled her eyes. "Well, I didn't come to play with you stupid babies. I came to get Cynthia. I left her here yesterday. And Aunt Didi told my daddy she had a surprise for me."

Angelica looked around the yard.

"Where is Aunt Didi, anyway? I want my surprise now!"

Just then Didi came around the side of the house. She was carrying Dil and a big box covered with colorful pictures and labels. "Hi, everybody!" she called. Didi plopped Dil down on Dactar's cushy new baby seat. "How's it coming along, Stu?"

Stu shook his head. "Dactar's still grounded. I've tried everything. It would take somebody smarter than me to figure out what the problem is."

Tommy frowned. Who could be smarter than his daddy?

"Don't worry, Stu," Didi said smiling. "Soon you'll have two geniuses to help you."

"Huh?" said Stu, surprised. "Who?"

"Why, Tommy and Dil, of course!" Didi giggled.

Stu still looked baffled.

"Well, maybe they're not quite geniuses

yet," Didi said, "but Tommy and Dil might be someday, thanks to this."

She showed everyone the box she had been carrying. Stu stared at a picture of a head with a big pink brain printed on the side of the box. "'Build a Bigger Baby Brain,'" he read out loud. "We're going to make the boys' brains bigger?"

The other babies gasped and looked at Tommy in dismay.

"What's that mean, Tommy?" Chuckie gulped.

Tommy shook his head, looking worried. "I don't know, but it can't be good!"

"Stu, isn't it exciting?" Didi said as she tapped the lid of the box. "This box is going to make our boys smarter!"

CHAPTER 2

As Didi started pulling things out of the box, she explained, "Dr. Lipschitz spoke at my Power Mommies lunch today. He showed us all his different smart-baby kits. Let's see, there's the George Washington Leadership Kit, an Isadora Duncan Dance Kit, the Einstein Energy Kit . . ."

Didi smiled down at Tommy and Dil. "Naturally, I got the superdeluxe model. Only the best for our boys!"

Tommy heaved a sigh of relief. "I guess getting a big brain isn't so scary after all," he said to his friends. "My mommy wouldn't get one for me if it was bad."

"Oh, yeah?" Angelica narrowed her eyes at Tommy. "What about that cod-liver baby food she got you?"

"Spike liked it," Tommy said.

Meanwhile, Stu was reading the small print on the box. "Let's see . . . it says here that you can make your baby's brain grow by using Dr. Lipschitz's 'Approach of Total Engrossment.' Sounds interesting."

"When is your brain gonna start growing, Tommy?" Lil asked eagerly.

Tommy felt his head. "Soon, I guess."

"Which kit did you get, Deed?" Stu asked.

"Well, I know how much you admire him," Didi said. "So I picked . . . the Leonardo da Vinci Renaissance Man Kit!"

Stu's eyes opened wide. "Leonardo da Vinci? He's my hero! The man was a genius!" he spluttered. "You mean to tell me that you think Tommy and Dil can become just as smart as da Vinci from a kit?"

Didi nodded.

"How does it work?" Lulu asked.

"Everything we need is right here," Didi said, patting the box. "If we surround Tommy and Dil with things about Leonardo—pictures of his inventions, copies of his paintings, the sights and sounds of sixteenth-century Italy—the boys will pick all of it up naturally."

Tommy turned to his friends, looking worried. "Did you hear that? To get my brain to grow, I gots to pick up lots of stuff. What if it's too heavy?"

"I'll help you, Tommy," Chuckie said, flexing his arms.

Angelica rolled her eyes again. "I'm tired of talking about your stupid brain," she said. "I want my surprise."

Angelica walked over to Didi. "I can't help pick up Italy," she told Didi, pointing to her bandage. "I've got a boo-boo. A boo-boo, 'member?"

"Pick up Italy? No, no, honey," Didi said. "Italy isn't something you pick up. It's the country where Leonardo da Vinci lived."

Lulu added, "Your aunt meant the boys will learn about Italy and be as smart as Leonardo da Vinci just by being around all the things in that box."

Stu looked up from reading the instruction book. "Listen to this," he said. "It says here that people can learn to speak other languages in their sleep, just by listening to recordings of people talking."

Didi nodded. "Maybe Tommy and Dil can learn to speak Italian just like Leonardo." She looked dreamy. "Imagine! Our boys, able to speak another language!"

"Maybe we should let those sprouts learn how to talk first," Grandpa Lou said.

"I can talk another langwich already, lots of 'em," Angelica bragged.

"Really, dear?" Didi smiled down at Angelica.

"Yeah," Angelica said. "Listen: Tacos! Moo Goo Gai Pan! French fries!"

"Um, that's wonderful, honey," Didi said.

"I know some too!" Kimi whispered to the babies. "*C'est la vie, ma chère.*"

Angelica frowned at her. "What's that mean?"

"I dunno," Kimi shrugged. "My mommy said it when I broke my oatmeal bowl."

Angelica glared at Kimi. "Well, that's not so hard. I can say it too." She cleared her throat. "Say-la-vee my chair!"

Grandpa Lou hooked a hand around his ear and looked over at Angelica in astonishment. "That's funny, I coulda sworn the sprout said, '*C'est la vie, ma chère.*'" He scratched his head. "Naw, that's plum crazy!"

"Why, Lou?" asked Lulu.

"Well, 'cause it's French for, 'That's life, my dear,'" Grandpa Lou explained. "It's kinda like saying, 'Don't worry about it, sugar-pie.'"

The other grown-ups blinked at him in surprise. "I picked up a little French in the war," Grandpa Lou boasted.

"I did too talk French," Angelica broke in, determined to show off. "See, I'll do it again. Say-la—" She forgot the rest and just growled, "Grrrrr!"

"Now, that's something different altogether, sprout," Grandpa Lou said, shaking his head. "In French, '*C'est la guerre*' means, 'That's war.'"

"Whatever," Angelica muttered.

"Well, anyway, the boys could pick up some Italian just by listening to this while they sleep," Didi said, holding up a CD.

Stu took the disc from her and leaned past Dil to pop it into Dactar's new CD player. A voice as smooth as silk purred softly in his ear. "*Buongiorno.* Good morning. *Come sta?* How are you? *Ho la matita verde*. I have a green pencil. . . ." Stu turned it off. "Well, at least the CD player works now," he said.

"That's nice, dear," Didi said. She was busy propping posters all around the backyard. "These are paintings Leonardo da Vinci made in Florence, Italy. I'll hang them in the boys' room later. Aren't they beautiful?"

Stu nodded absently. He had just spotted the drawings of helicopters, diving suits, and other inventions in the kit. "Check this out, Deed," he said, waving a picture of a funny-looking parachute. "Da Vinci was hundreds of years ahead of his time."

Then Stu sighed. "His inventions inspired me to become an inventor myself. And if only I was as smart as da Vinci, I'd have Dactar fixed up in no time."

Tommy nudged Chuckie. "I wish we could find that smart da Binky guy for my daddy. Then Dactar could fly."

Chuckie nodded. "But it sounds like da Binky is far away."

"Binky!" Dil gurgled. All he had to do was hear the word and he wanted one.

Tommy popped a Binky in his brother's mouth, and Dil smiled up at him happily.

"Da Vinci was smart, all right!" Stu was still talking about his hero. "He was one of history's greatest painters, an inventor and a scientist and an architect and a—"

"All right, already," Angelica said, shrugging. "He was a big shot. I get it."

"Yup, da Vinci was a real Renaissance man," Stu added.

The babies watched as Stu picked up his diagram of the Dactar flying machine. "Next to Leonardo's inventions, I guess mine seem pretty silly." Stu sighed, tossing the paper into Dactar's cabin.

"Aw, son, don't worry yourself about

some guy who lived hundreds of years ago," Grandpa Lou told Stu. "There's lots of other things you should be worrying about, like—"

Suddenly Grandpa Lou's nose wrinkled like he'd just smelled something bad. He sniffed the air. "Maybe we should eat out tonight. Whatever you got cookin' in there doesn't smell too good," he said.

"It's my cauliflower–blue cheese stew," Stu said. His eyes grew wide, and he started racing for his lab. "I left it on the Bunsen burner in my workshop hours ago!"

"Goodness!" Didi headed indoors. "It's probably boiled over!"

Lulu ran after her. "I'll help clean up!"

"They'll just make a bigger mess unless I show 'em how it's done," Grandpa Lou complained.

A minute later it was quiet and the babies were alone in the backyard. Didi, Lulu, Stu, and Grandpa Lou all thought one of the other grown-ups was still watching the babies.

Just then the babies heard an odd voice. "*Dove sono?* Where am I? *Sono qui.* I am here."

CHAPTER 3

The babies looked around. "Who said that?" Chuckie asked, looking nervous.

Everyone had forgotten that Stu had put a CD in the Dactar mobile—and that Dil was still in there. But Dil liked pushing buttons and he had just punched the one that turned on the CD player.

"*Sei qui*. You are here."

"It's Dactar!" Chuckie finally figured. "Listen! He's talking some weird dinosaur langwich."

The babies stared nervously at the flying machine.

"*Il ragazzo è qui*. The boy is here. *La*

ragazza è qui. The girl is here. *Il bambino è qui.* The baby is here."

"Uh-oh," Lil said. "He knows we're here."

"So maybe we better get outta here," Phil added.

Then Tommy saw something move inside the flying machine's cockpit.

"Ooomeenoo," came Dil's voice, babbling faintly.

"Dil!" Tommy gasped. "We can't leave him!"

"*Venite qui.* Come here," the voice continued.

"We better do what Dactar says," Tommy said. "He's got Dil!"

The babies clambered into the Dactar mobile.

"*Voresti essere il mio amico?* Will you be my friend?"

Chuckie heaved a sigh. Even Angelica looked relieved. "I guess Dactar's not gonna eat us. Let's get out now," she said.

26

But the others were being lulled by the soft voice. Soon their eyes were slipping shut as they listened to the silky sounds.

"Oh, brother," Angelica said as she rolled her eyes. "You better not go to sleep," she warned the babies. "You heard what Aunt Didi said. If somebody talks to you when you're sleepin', that means you're gonna talk just like them when you wake up."

But the voice coming from Dactar had the same gentle tones as a lullaby. Finally, Angelica closed her eyes too.

"*Arrivederci*. Farewell."

If the babies' eyes had been open, they would have seen Dil lean over just then and poke another button—a big red button, just like the one on Stu's remote control.

"Boootoooo!" Dil cooed.

There was a loud grinding sound, and smoke began puffing out of the back of the flying machine. The noise woke

Angelica and the babies. They opened their eyes to see thick smoke all around them.

"What's happening, Tommy?" Chuckie wailed.

"I think we're taking off!" Tommy shouted above the noise of the engine.

Dactar shuddered and groaned. The flying machine seemed to tilt and spin. The babies grabbed on to each other.

"Hang on!" Tommy yelled. That's when the engine gave another groan—*uurrrgggh*—and suddenly stopped.

For a second, it felt like the Dactar flying machine was falling, but before anyone could get too scared, the machine landed with a loud CRUNCH! and a THUMP!

When the smoke cleared, they were safely on the ground. Everyone tumbled out of the machine. As Angelica and Tommy took Dil and his baby seat out, Dactar was still talking.

"*Benvenuti in Italiaaaaa.* Wellllcommme to IIIItaaaalllyyyy . . ." The voice slowed down before coming to a final stop.

"Uh-oh. Dactar doesn't sound too good," said Phil.

"Hey!" said Angelica. She kicked Dactar's tire. "Wake up!"

"I don't think he's sleepin', Angelica," Lil shook her head. "I think we busteded him."

Lil pointed. Sure enough, one of Dactar's wings was broken and flapping loosely in the breeze.

"Oh, no!" Tommy cried, thinking about how upset his dad would be. Then, to make matters worse, one of the metal gears fell out of Dactar's engine with a clang.

"Get it!" Kimi yelled. "It's gonna roll down the hill!"

"Hill?" Tommy said.

The babies looked around. They were

standing on the top of a steep, grassy hill. The gear rolled all the way down into a river, then disappeared with a loud *KERPLOP!*

"Uh, Tommy?" Chuckie edged closer to his best friend. "This doesn't eggsackly look like your backyard anymore."

From where they stood, Angelica and the babies could see a small city not far away. The city was filled with sturdy-looking, old-fashioned buildings topped with domes and bell towers. Small stone bridges crisscrossed a river that snaked through the town.

"Where are we?" Kimi wondered.

Angelica stomped over to Dil and glared at him. "Where did that little diaper bag land us this time?" she snapped.

"Well, Dactar said, 'Welcome to Little-ee' just before he got quiet. Maybe that's where we are," Tommy figured.

"Well, I don't like it here," said

Angelica. "It looks like a dump. And I left Cynthia back home. So I say we leave right NOW!"

"But we can't go anywhere until we fix Dactar for my dad," Tommy said.

Chuckie nodded. "We might get into trouble."

"'Specially you, Angelica," Kimi said. "You were closest to where he got broked."

Angelica narrowed her eyes. "I didn't do nuthin'." She pointed at Dil. "It was that poop-factory that did it!"

"Yucky," Dil burbled in reply.

Tommy thought for a moment. "Hey, da Binky could fix Dactar. My dad said so, 'member?"

Lil nodded. "Yeah. An' your Mommy said da Binky was in Little-ee."

Tommy reached into the flying machine for the diagram Stu had tossed inside. "Da Binky might need this pitcher of Dactar," Tommy said, tucking the sheet into his diaper. "C'mon guys, let's go find him!"

The babies started walking down the hill. Luckily, the baby seat Stu had built for the Dactar machine was the deluxe model. It had wheels that flipped down when it was detached from the flying machine, and the baby seat now became a stroller that Tommy and the others could push.

"C'mon, Angelica," Tommy called as the babies marched off.

"No way," Angelica muttered. "I'm staying right here. That place doesn't look fun to me."

She plopped herself down on the grass. Just then she spotted an open carriage driven by four horses riding up to the city gate.

Angelica perked up. "Hey! Lookit that!"

A lady sat in the carriage. She wore a fancy long dress covered with jewels that flashed and sparkled in the sun. A moment later the guards waved the carriage past, and it disappeared into the town.

Angelica liked that dress. It would be perfect for Cynthia. Suddenly she had an idea—maybe she could find a dress like that in the town. And maybe one for her, too. She jumped up and called out to the others. "Hey! Wait for me!"

CHAPTER 4

At the bottom of the hill, Angelica and the babies could see a stout man carrying a heavy club standing guard at the town gate. He snapped to attention when he saw them approach.

"Who goes there?" he yelled out in a nervous voice.

"Tommy, he's talking that funny Dactar langwich," Chuckie whispered.

"And we understand him," Tommy whispered back.

"Who goes there?" the guard shouted again, and squinted at them. "Who dares approach the gates of Florence?"

"Four ants?" Phil said, looking interested. "Where? I love ants!"

Tommy shouted at the guard. "Hi! We're looking for da Binky. Does he live here?"

The guard just looked puzzled. "Huh? Who?"

"Maybe he can't hear from so far away," Tommy said. The babies moved closer to the gate.

"Halt! I command you—oh!" The guard blinked when he saw Tommy up close. He called up to another guard in the watchtower. "Do not worry, my friend. It is only a little *bambino*." Then he saw the others. "Oh, there are seven of them!"

"Hey! *Bambino* means 'baby'!" Angelica snapped, remembering what Dactar had said. "You better not be calling me that."

The guard smiled. "What are you doing outside the city? Can you not see that it is going to rain?" He shooed Angelica and the others inside the gate. "Quickly now, or you will be wet!" he warned.

Angelica and the babies walked down a stone street, pushing Dil in his stroller and looking around. Stone buildings crowded both sides of the narrow road.

"People here dress funny," Lil said, staring at the caps and poofy hats the men wore, the long aprons of the women, and the stiff ruffled collars on some of the people passing by.

There were people everywhere, and the sound of voices laughing, talking, and yelling at one another echoed off the stone walls. Horses and goats clopped loudly on the streets.

"It's so noisy!" Kimi said.

"An' smelly!" said Angelica. She wrinkled her nose at the dung lumped on the road. "Don't they ever wash the streets around here?"

Just then a flood of water came flying

out of a window above them. It landed on Angelica in a soapy splash.

"Hey!" Angelica glared from under her wet bangs. "Cut that out!"

A head poked out from the window. "Oh! Excuse me, *bambina!*" A boy not much older than Angelica smiled down at them, his eyes twinkling.

"I am not a *bambina!*" Angelica shrieked. "And you are *not* 'scused!"

The boy's head disappeared, and a minute later he opened the door in front of them. He held out a rag toward Angelica. "Forgive me, I beg you!" The boy introduced himself. "I am Matteo, at your service, *signorina.*"

Angelica snatched the rag and tried to dry off her dripping pigtails. "What's that mean?" she asked suspiciously.

"I promise to perform whatever services I can to make up for my poor manners," Matteo said.

"You don't hafta do that," Kimi said. "It was just an ax-dent."

Angelica glared at her. "Who asked you, shortie?" Then she turned to Matteo and her face brightened. "I know what you can do! Get me a fancy dress. Plus one for Cynthia. With jewels and sparkly things on it."

Matteo shook his head. "I am but a poor servant and cannot buy such things. But I will think of some deed I can do for you, I promise."

"A deed?" said Angelica, making a face.

"That's nice of you," Chuckie said.

"It is not nice, it is a matter of honor." When he saw their puzzled looks, Matteo drew himself up proudly and explained, "I am honor-bound to make amends. I should have looked below before I emptied my master's bathwater."

"That's right!" Angelica snapped, and then realized what Matteo had said. "Yuck! I've got somebody's dirty water all over me!"

Matteo's eyes started to twinkle again. "But at least it was not the toilet water! That is emptied out the window too, you know!" He laughed at the look on Angelica's face.

Angelica fumed. Then she sniffed the air and held her nose. "Maybe you should have used some water yourself. You could use a bath!"

The boy looked surprised. "But I had my wash just a fortnight ago," he said. "For me, there will not come another for many weeks."

"Weeks?" Chuckie was shocked.

"I see you are surprised that we bathe so often in my master's house," the boy said. "Only the best families and their servants wash so much. Yes, we are considered very modern, even for this year of 1505. We beat our clothing as much as once a week to remove the dirt and bugs."

Angelica looked disgusted. "Bugs?"

"Lots of bugs and no baths," Phil said, sighing. "I like it here."

Matteo laughed again.

Tommy smiled. "Nice meetin' you, Matteo. But we gots to go and find da Binky."

"Da Binky? Oh—Leonardo da Vinci! Then you must look in the Piazza della Signorina," Matteo said. "It is the most beautiful plaza in all of Italy, and many artists gather there."

Tommy was excited. Surely da Binky would be there! He grabbed Dil's stroller. "C'mon, guys!"

"We don't know where that pizza place is," Chuckie said.

"I will show you where," Matteo said. "My master has called for me to assist him in his work at a building near the piazza," he added, "so it is no trouble."

"If it's no trouble, that doesn't count as

the service you owe me," Angelica warned him.

"Who's your master, Matteo?" Tommy asked.

"I am honored by being a runner in the house of Piero Soderini," Matteo said solemnly. He explained that runners were the lowest of all servants, made to do any chore that came along.

Angelica snorted. "That doesn't sound like an honor to me."

"You are wrong. It is an honor to serve the leader of the great council of Florence, even if he is a hard master," said Matteo. Just then a raindrop splashed him on the nose. "Come, we must hurry. A storm will soon reach the city!"

Angelica grumbled. "Why don't we stay here? I don't wanna get all wet"—she glared at Matteo—"again!"

Matteo pointed the way. "It is not far. And when the rain arrives you can take shelter in the church by the piazza, or in the Palazzo Vecchio. No one will notice you in the palace as long as you stay in the servants' area."

"*Palace?*" Suddenly Angelica perked up and her eyes gleamed. "Did you say 'palace'?"

Matteo nodded. "The Palazzo is a palace, although you will not find kings or princesses there. Florence is now free from them," he said proudly.

But Angelica didn't hear what Matteo said. "A palace! Get moving, slowpokes!" she shouted as she hurried off in the direction Matteo had pointed them. Matteo and the babies ran after her. It was hard keeping up.

"A palace is just the place for Princess Angelica Pickles," Angelica said to herself as she ran. Her lips curled into a smile. She would finally get exactly what she deserved!

CHAPTER 5

"Wow! Look at all the peoples!" Chuckie stared around the piazza.

The group had finally reached the great plaza. It turned out to be a big, open square in the center of the city.

There were people selling glass goblets and pots, weavers crafting yards of cloth, and even a man building a large wooden bucket.

"How will we ever find da Binky?" Tommy wondered, looking around. All he could see were people's knees.

"I will help you—" Matteo began to say, when suddenly a voice rang out across the square. "Matteo! I see you there, boy. Come quickly, I need you!"

The babies looked up. A man was leaning out a window in a big building nearby. He shook a finger angrily. "Hurry, boy, or things will go badly for you!"

Matteo gulped. "It is my master, Piero Soderini."

"He sure sounds grouchy," Kimi said with a shudder. She felt sorry for their new friend.

Matteo looked sadly down at the babies. "I must leave you now, but later I will help again."

He showed the babies a large church at the edge of the square. "We will meet there later, when my work is done. *Ciao!*"

The babies watched as Matteo ran off. Without him, the square suddenly seemed even larger and the people all too busy to help a bunch of babies.

"What'll we do now?" Chuckie asked in a worried voice.

Just then Dil started to cry. "Unngee!" he wailed.

"Uh-oh," Tommy said. "We better find Dil a bottle fast!"

"I'm hungry too," said Phil.

"An' me," Lil agreed.

Then the twins spotted something over in a corner of the square. Inside a long passageway filled with statues, a woman sat milking a cow. A basket of bread sat on the ground beside her.

"Let's ask her for some food," Lil said.

"Lil and me will get some milk for Dil," Phil said, grabbing Dil's stroller. "You guys go find da Binky."

"Yeah, and we'll see you later at that church place," Lil said. She looked hungrily at the bread and rubbed her tummy. "C'mon, Phil!"

"Thanks, guys. We'll be right back!"

Tommy called as the twins wheeled Dil over to the lady with the cow. He watched as the lady playfully squirted some milk at Dil, who giggled in delight.

"You think Dil will be okay?" Tommy asked.

"Sure, sure," Angelica said, sighing. "Now, let's go look for my palace!"

Tommy frowned. "Huh? We're looking for da Binky."

"Yeah, right . . . ," Angelica said as she rolled her eyes. "If he's so smart, I bet he's in the palace. So come on, let's go."

Plopping himself down on the base of a statue, Chuckie said, "I gots to rest, Angelica. We walked too far already."

Angelica scowled. "I wanna see the palace! Come on."

But the babies weren't listening; they were staring up at the statue that towered over Chuckie.

"Look, he lost his diapie!" Kimi giggled.

The statue was of a boy not much older than Matteo, but much taller. Its stern face gazed off across the piazza.

"You like our *David*, eh?" asked a woman passing by. In her arms was a big basket filled with clucking ducks. "He is ready to fight the giant Goliath, no?"

Chuckie nodded, even though he thought David looked big enough to be a giant himself. "Who made him?"

The woman smiled. "Michelangelo made the *David*."

The ducks clucked loudly, and the woman hurried off, calling *"Ciao!"*

"That Milk-and-angel man sure is a good statue-maker," Chuckie said. "but he's got a funny name."

"Okay, you rested long enough, Chuckie!" Angelica snapped. "Let's go!"

Just then a skinny man rushed up to the statue, carrying an armload of scrolls. He stared down his nose at Chuckie. "Out of my way!" he commanded, wiggling his fingers. "It is my custom to read here each midday."

Chuckie jumped aside as the man clambered up onto the base of the statue.

"The supreme poet Ariosto is here, to please your ear with verses and a voice so clear!" the skinny man shrieked over the noises of the crowd.

"It is Ariosto!" some of the townspeople murmured. Soon, a crowd gathered around the statue. Everyone seemed excited to hear him speak.

Ariosto cleared his throat and began to recite at the top of his voice:

"Of loves and ladies, knights and arms, I sing,
Of courtesies, and many a daring feat;
And from those ancient days my story brings . . ."

"Oooh, I like stories," Angelica said loudly, moving closer to hear. "Especially about knightses and ladies."

The poet glared at the interruption. He cleared his throat, mumbled a minute, and then picked up his poem again.

"Though many days no news of her had shown,
The beautiful Angelica is known . . ."

Angelica's jaw dropped.
"Angelica, that's you!" Kimi said in surprise.

CHAPTER 6

"Hey!" Angelica gasped. "He's talking about me! I'm famous!"

The poet had stopped reciting and was frowning down at Angelica. "Shhhh! The great Ariosto is speaking," the poet said. "I am about to recite the best part. The part where Angelica flees to her palazzo and—"

"Palazzo? That's the palace, right?" Angelica interrupted excitedly. She turned to the other babies. "See! That palace really is mine."

"The palace belongs to the maiden Angelica," Ariosto snapped. He was reciting the tale of Orlando and Angelica of Cathay, which was famous in Florence.

"That's what I said! I'm Angelica, so it's my palace," Angelica said, poking Ariosto in the leg. "Go on, talk some more about me an' my palace."

"Enough!" Ariosto looked around at the crowd and whined. "I am an artist! I cannot work like this!" Then he stomped away.

A groan went up from the crowd, who had eagerly awaited the exciting part of the poem. The townspeople scowled angrily at the babies.

"We must find our entertainment elsewhere," growled a dirty-looking man in the crowd. "Let us make those little ones dance or jest for us."

Chuckie gulped. "But I dunno how to dance."

"We can't really walk yet," Tommy added.

The crowd didn't seem to care. They began to chant. "Dance, jesters, dance!"

"Uh . . . look! He's over there! He's gonna say his poem now!" Angelica suddenly shouted. She pointed off to the other side of the square. "Hurry, or you'll miss it!"

The crowd's chant instantly changed. "Ariosto! Ariosto!" they yelled instead, surging in the direction Angelica had pointed.

"I just made that up," Angelica told the babies. "Let's get outta here!"

She ran toward a building made of huge stone blocks. The babies followed as fast as they could.

"This place is so big, they'll never find us!" Angelica said as she tugged at one of the doors.

The babies stared up at the building. A tall tower on top pointed at the sky like a long, skinny finger. The place seemed like an imposing fortress. "It doesn't look like a good place for babies," Chuckie said worriedly. "Maybe there's a monster inside."

"Don't worry, Chuckie," Kimi said. "Monsters only live in closets and under beds."

But she grabbed his hand, anyway, and held on tight.

As the babies looked up at the towering structure, afraid to go in, thunder rumbled loudly from the clouds above. A streak of lightning shot across the sky. Seconds later, rain started pouring down.

"C'mon!" Tommy shouted. "My mommy says not to be outside when it's thunnerin' and frightening."

The moment they were inside, Tommy suddenly remembered something. "Dil!" Tommy cried. "He's out there with Phil and Lil! They're gonna get wet, and Dil will be scared."

"Don't be dumb," Angelica snorted. "They're with that nice lady and the cow. They won't even get wet, 'cause she was inside, by the statue."

"But can we find 'em again?" Tommy asked.

"They'll be at that church place later, 'member?'" Angelica said. She looked down the long, stone hallway. "Now, let's see if there's a back door so we can sneak out without anybody seeing us."

The babies walked up and down the dimly lit stone hallways and stairs. Finally, a tall wooden door blocked their way. The babies could hear a voice muttering on the other side of the half-open door.

"What's that?" Chuckie whispered.

"Maybe it's somebody who can show us the way out," Kimi nervously suggested.

Tommy took a deep breath and said, "C'mon, guys, we're goin' in!"

He pushed the door all the way open. On the other side was a huge room. The walls soared high up to a raised portion of the ceiling, and marble sculptures stood in the corners. Wooden benches lined the walls.

But the babies weren't looking at any of that. They were staring at something crouched in the middle of the room. It had a cape that trailed over its back to the floor in dusty black folds.

"Wh-wh-what is it?" Chuckie gulped. "A monster?"

Tommy squinted to get a closer look. Then he saw a smear of paint on the cape and brightened. "It's da Binky!"

CHAPTER 7

"I AM NOT DA VINCI!"

The second Tommy spoke, the thing spun around and roared.

It was a really loud roar, but it didn't scare Tommy. He could see that it was just a man wearing a funny faded red hat that flopped around on his head like a deflated balloon.

"I am MICHELANGELO!" the man shouted. Then he noticed something. "Why, you are only *bambini*," he added in a softer voice.

"I AM NOT A BABY!" Angelica roared.

The man looked startled, then began to laugh. "I see that you are just as fierce as me, eh, *bambi*—"—he shut his mouth quickly when Angelica narrowed her eyes—"I mean *signorina*."

All at once Michelangelo noticed that Chuckie and Kimi were still huddled behind Tommy. "Ah! I did not mean to scare you, little ones. It is just that I cannot bear to hear that name, Leonardo da Vinci!"

Michelangelo patted Tommy on the head. "But you could not have known that. I am sorry for shouting at you."

Chuckie and Kimi returned his smile. Tommy nodded and toddled farther into the room. He noticed some papers scattered on the floor near some pens, ink bottles, and broken sticks of black and red chalk.

"See, guys, he's not scary. He likes to color too. Lookit all this stuff," Tommy told the other babies.

"Do not look at my poor scribbles," Michelangelo said, sweeping one of the papers off the floor and crumpling it into a ball. "I do not like drawing or painting—such art is so flat and dull."

"But this is nice!" Tommy held up one of the papers to show the others. "You're the bestest drawer I ever saw."

Even Angelica had to agree. She stared at the picture of some men climbing the banks of a river. "Yeah, they look really real."

"You are kind. But no, at art such as this, I do not care to be the best," Michelangelo said. "No, I am the master of sculpting. Truly the 'bestest,' as you say!"

Michelangelo saw the babies' puzzled faces and explained. "I carve the stone for statues, you understand?"

Angelica suddenly remembered the statue in the plaza outside. "Oh, I get it! You're that Milk-and-angel man," she said.

Now Michelangelo looked puzzled. "No, you do not say it right," he said, frowning.

"You will call me Michelangelo, please."

Kimi, Chuckie, Tommy, and Angelica nodded. "Milk-and-angel," they recited together. Michelangelo sighed.

"Uh, you guys? We gots to go," Tommy reminded the babies. "We still gots to look for . . . you-know-who." He tried not to say 'da Binky' again.

"Why do we gots to find, uh, you-know-who, anyways? What's wrong with him?" Angelica asked, pointing at Michelangelo. "He's some kinda artist too."

"But my daddy said you-know-who was a painter. Milk-and-angel said he's not a painter even though he's got paint on his coat," Tommy said.

"I'm sure he could paint somethin' if we asked him," Angelica insisted. But Michelangelo overheard her and shook his head.

"I do not like painting, but that is all anyone wants from me," he said sadly. He waved a hand at a big blank wall on one side of the room. "They tell me to paint a picture here. But it would be better if they would let me make a statue instead. That would be my masterpiece."

"Who's Mister Peas?" Kimi wondered.

Michelangelo laughed out loud. "No, little one. A masterpiece is not a man. It is the work of art one thinks is the very best," he explained.

Then Michelangelo seemed to remember something and looked gloomy again. "And when the Pope calls me to Rome, I know he will tell me I should stop thinking about statues and paint some ceilings for him instead."

Michelangelo spat on the floor. "Paint— bah! I hate to paint! And all he will want are little angels."

He stared at them glumly. Then he blinked. At that moment, sunlight was beginning to struggle through the clouds outside, and one bright beam streamed down in a sparkle of gold. It danced around Tommy's head like a halo.

"You are an angel, in truth!" Michelangelo clasped his hands together joyfully. "For if I must paint angels, here is my inspiration!"

Michelangelo grabbed a piece of paper and a stick of red chalk.

"If I make many sketches now for the ceiling, I will finish sooner and can begin sculpting once more," he said. He started scribbling, glancing at Tommy.

"You will pose for me," he commanded. "I will draw my cartoon for the ceiling, and you will be my angel."

"Hey, cartoons! I love cartoons," Chuckie said.

Angelica stared at the artist in surprise. "You have cartoons here? I don't even see a TV!"

Michelangelo looked confused. "I do

not know this TV you speak of. Perhaps you do not understand?"

"Before artists like myself make a great painting," he explained as he drew, "they make many little sketches first to see which idea is best. One of these will become the cartoon. That is what we call the drawing that is the same size as the finished painting."

Michelangelo looked up from his sketch of Tommy. "My cartoon of your friend will be for the Pope's ceiling. But I must also make a cartoon for my fresco, my wall painting, here."

He gestured at the empty wall on one side of the hall. Then he turned his attention back to Tommy, who squirmed under the artist's intense gaze. "Sometimes it takes many months for the cartoon. But do not worry, *bambino*, the cartoon I'm drawing of you will only take one day."

"No way!" Tommy shook his head. "We

gots to get back to Phil and Lil and Dil as soon as we can."

"And find da Binky," Chuckie added.

Michelangelo clapped his hands over his ears. "The *bambino,* he speaks that cursed name again!"

Angelica poked him in the arm. "Hey! If you don't like this Binky guy, that means you know him, right? We gots to see him, or these stupid babies won't help me find somethin' I'm looking for."

"I know Leonardo da Vinci, yes," Michelangelo said frowning.

The babies gasped.

"The council of Florence has asked us each to paint something . . . to make us work harder," Michelangelo continued, grumbling.

He laughed loudly again. "And they are right! Because I do not care for this Leonardo da Vinci—no!—his fresco cannot be better than mine!"

"Boy, you sure don't like da Binky," Angelica said.

"Like him?" Michelangelo snapped. "I will never forgive him. Never!"

CHAPTER 8

"But why don't you like . . . uh . . . you-know-who?" Tommy asked.

Michelangelo took a deep breath. "It was da Vinci who helped the people put my *David* down in the piazza. For that, I will never forgive him or those others on the committee!"

Tommy was puzzled. "But it looks nice out there, and everybodies can see him."

Michelangelo quivered with rage. "No! My statue was meant to go up. Up!" He flapped a hand in the air, toward the top of the building. "I sculpt him to be seen from far below. Now, on the ground, the head and hands, they are too big. It is grotesque!"

The babies shrugged. Most people looked like giants to them, anyway.

Michelangelo groaned. "You do not understand. For many years Leonardo da Vinci has been the pride of Italy." He thumped his chest. "The people think he is greater even than Michelangelo."

Angelica smirked. "You're just jealous."

"Jealous?" Michelangelo scratched his head, then shrugged. "Perhaps. But when people say I should be like him, it makes me crazy!"

Michelangelo shook his head and picked up his paper and charcoal. He was ready to start drawing Tommy again.

Just then the babies heard a distant rumble of thunder. Tommy looked up in dismay. "It's thunnerin' again," Tommy said worriedly. "Dil's a-scared of thunner."

"Maybe Phil and Lil took Dil to that church place," Kimi suggested.

"Let's go back there," said Tommy.

Michelangelo looked up from his sketch. "The church across the piazza? The city council has given me keys so I may use it for my studio." He looked at Tommy slyly. "Perhaps I will take you there later if you pose for me now, eh?"

But before Tommy could say anything, Angelica had an idea.

"Hold on a minute," she said to Michelangelo. "First I wanna see the palace. If you show us where it is, maybe we can stick around awhile and these stupid babies can be your angels."

"Angelica!" Tommy yelled.

But Michelangelo was looking confused. "The palazzo? But this is the palazzo—the Palazzo Vecchio."

Angelica couldn't believe her ears. She looked around. "What kind of junky palace is this? Where's the throne? An' the jewels? An' the people to wait on the

Princess Angelica?" she cried.

Michelangelo started to laugh. Then he jumped up and bounded across the room. "Come, I will show you treasures!"

Angelica and the babies trailed the artist out of the big room and down a long hallway lined with many doors. He stopped in front of one.

"Now, to find the keys the council entrusted to me," he muttered, before locating an iron ring hidden in the folds of his cloak. He plucked a gold key from the ring.

Unlocking the door, Michelangelo dramatically announced, with a sweep of his hand, "Behold! The Lily Chamber of the Palazzo Vecchio!"

The Lily Chamber was filled with rich decorations and elegant furniture. The ceilings and walls were covered in paintings and fancy carvings. Small tables were tucked into corners, displaying jeweled boxes and other fancy knick-knacks.

The babies gasped. Even Angelica was struck dumb—almost. "Ooooh!" she exclaimed. "Look!"

Angelica had spotted a gorgeous china doll with fancy braids. The doll sat propped in a silk-covered chair, dressed in a long gown covered with sparkly jewels— just like the one worn by the lady in the carriage.

"Many of the treasures here come from the Palazzo Medici," Michelangelo explained. "The Medici family once ruled the city like royalty. Perhaps they will one day return to Florence. But for now, they are gone, and the family's riches are kept here."

"Yeah, yeah," Angelica snapped. She was itching to get at those riches herself, especially the doll. Her eyes narrowed as she tried to shove past Michelangelo. "Outta my way!"

But Michelangelo quickly slammed the door shut and turned the gold key in its lock. Then he dangled the key in the air. "Not so fast, *signorina!*" he said, wagging a finger. "These riches belong to the Republic of Florence."

"Says who? Finder's keepers!" Angelica tried to pull open the door. "Gimme that key!"

Tommy tugged at Angelica's sleeve. "C'mon, Angelica. He says you can't play with the doll. So let's go look for Dil and da Binky."

Angelica ignored him and glared at Michelangelo. Michelangelo smiled and leaned back against the door, swinging the golden key back and forth.

"Perhaps if the *bambino* stays to let me paint him, I will tell you where to find Leonardo da Vinci. And I will give you this key so you may play with the doll you like so much," he said.

Angelica's eyes gleamed.

"It must be for only a little while because a committee for the council meets soon in the chamber," Michelangelo added, then he grinned widely. "But it is a fair trade, no?"

Angelica really wanted to play with that doll. "Let me think. . . ."

Tommy folded his arms and planted his feet. "No! I wanna leave!" he yelled. He wanted to find Dil and fix Dactar, not stay and pose for a dumb picture.

"Me too!" Chuckie said.

Kimi shook a finger at Angelica. "Tommy doesn't have to be anybody's angel!"

Angelica squinted her eyes. If Tommy didn't pose, she'd never get close to that doll. "You gots to, Tommy! Or—"

She was going to say "or else." But then she thought of something even better. "Or Milk-and-angel won't tell us where da

Binky is," she finished. "You heard him. He knows da Binky. An' he can help us find Dil, too, 'cause he gots keys to that church."

Michelangelo dangled his key ring once more.

Tommy thought about it. How else was he going to find Dil and da Binky? "Well . . . maybe we could stay a little bit," he said. "But only if we look for Dil right after and Milk-and-angel promises to tell us where da Binky is."

Angelica turned to Michelangelo and smiled smugly. "You've got a deal!"

CHAPTER 9

A few minutes later, Tommy was sitting on a big chair, trying to look angelic. Kimi and Chuckie were busy coloring with Michelangelo's chalks.

Michelangelo handed Angelica the gold key and waved her away impatiently. He began scribbling on a piece of paper, making a cartoon of Tommy with a piece of charcoal. "It is no good to work here," he was mumbling. "The light is bad."

"I'm just gonna go play with that doll," Angelica said loudly, although no one was paying attention to her.

Soon she was unlocking the door to the

Lily Chamber. "At last!" Angelica sighed gleefully. There was the beautiful doll in her gorgeous sparkly dress.

Angelica slammed the door shut and ran to pick up the doll. "You're MINE!" Angelica told her. She pulled the doll off her chair and danced around the room with it. Then she stopped and frowned, remembering what Michelangelo had said about the doll being the property of the Republic. "But that mean ol' council isn't gonna let me take you."

Angelica smiled slyly. "But this is Angelica's palace, so everything here should belong to me. An' I just gots to sneak you out!"

Angelica looked around and spotted a window. She ran over and peeked through the narrow opening. It looked like the rain had almost stopped. The window was just a foot above the ground. The bushes below would cushion her fall.

"I'll hide you by Dactar and be back before Milk-and-angel and those stupid babies know I'm gone," Angelica muttered to the doll.

Angelica dragged one of the smaller, velvet-covered chairs over to the window. She was halfway out, her feet and the doll dangling inside the Lily Chamber, when the door burst open. A crowd of men wearing funny short skirts and high ruffled collars poured into the room, talking loudly. One of them carried a small, pug-faced dog.

Matteo was there too, carrying some papers.

"I say again, if only the heavens would grant us a sign," a tall man was saying. "A sign to tell us what to do in our hour of need."

When everyone saw Angelica hanging half out the window, they all stopped short. Even the dog looked surprised.

The tall man stepped forward. He had dark hair, a dark beard, and a dark expression on his face. "STOP!" he bellowed.

Angelica was so shocked that she fell back into the room and onto the chair.

"Thief!" the man shouted angrily. "You are under arrest!"

Angelica gulped and hugged the doll. The men glaring at her looked pretty mad. She needed a miracle to get out of this one!

Suddenly the sun broke through the clouds outside the window. A rainbow filled the sky behind Angelica's head. The men gasped at Angelica in awestruck wonder. "It is a sign!" the tall man told the others. "A truly wondrous sign! The small one must be the wise one we seek!"

CHAPTER 10

Now Angelica was surprised by the way she was being treated. These guys clearly thought she was a big, important somebody. She batted her eyelashes and smiled sweetly. "How ya doin'?"

"She looks kindly at us!" The tall man said, sweeping into a deep bow before Angelica. "I am humbled that you have forgiven my oafish ways! It is another sign of your wisdom and greatness!"

All the other men bowed low too. All except for Matteo, who was trying to stifle a laugh.

"I get it," Angelica said to herself. "They

figgered out I'm Princess Angelica!"

Her lips curled into an even bigger smile. This was gonna be good!

"We are ready to listen to your wise words," the tall man said. He glared at Matteo and snapped his fingers. "You beetle-brained knot-head! Present us to the wise one, churlish boy!"

Matteo's grin disappeared. Angelica could tell he was a little afraid of the man.

"Hey, cut that out!" Angelica snapped. She pointed at the mean man. "Be nice! The wise one says so."

Matteo smiled again and bowed before Angelica. "Exalted one, allow me to present my master, Piero Soderini, leader of the great council of Florence."

The tall man stepped forward proudly. "And these are the Eight on Security, a committee of the great council," Matteo continued. He first introduced the man with the dog as Machiavelli, a diplomat.

"You seem like a leader," Machiavelli told Angelica. The diplomat had a long, sad face and wore his hair in curls like the ribbons on a birthday present. "You know when to roar like the lion and when to sit silent as a fox."

"Whatever." Angelica yawned.

"We are here to discuss what we must do in case the French invade Florence," Piero explained. "Our city must not fall like so many other Italian cities!"

"I say we collect money to hire soldiers," Machiavelli said.

Angelica nodded. "That sounds good!"

"But where shall we get this money from, Niccolò Machiavelli? From the poor?" another of the men sneered.

"Like I said, that was a bad idea," Angelica said quickly. She was realizing that being a wise one was harder than she'd thought.

Just then the door opened. Two small

faces appeared in the opening.

"Hi, Angelica!" Kimi said. She looked in surprise at the crowd in the room. "We came to get you."

"That Milk-and-angel guy took Tommy to his studio at the church," said Chuckie, peeking over Kimi's shoulder. "He said it's got better lightbulbs or somethin'. Maybe Dil and Phil and Lil and Matteo are there too." Then Chuckie noticed Matteo. "Oh, hi," Chuckie said. "Whatcha doin'?"

Before Matteo could reply, Angelica stamped her foot. "Go away, you stupid babies," she hissed. "I was just about to get these guys to give me anything I want."

"Don't be so bossy, Angelica," Kimi snapped.

"Ahem!" Behind them, someone cleared his throat nosily. It was Piero.

"I crave your forgiveness for my presumption, wise one," he said, when he saw Angelica's beady-eyed glare. "But we ask for your counsel. You must answer."

Angelica folded her arms. "If I do, what'll you give me?"

Piero looked blank.

"Princesses like me don't give this wise stuff away for free, you know," Angelica told him.

"Princess?" Piero's eyes narrowed. "We have no such royalty in Florence. What do you mean?"

Angelica sighed loudly. "I mean . . . what kind of stuff will you give me if I help you out?"

"You mean a tribute of some kind?" Piero asked.

"Yeah!" Angelica said. "Like this doll for instance."

The men looked surprised.

"Certainly," Piero nodded. "It is yours!"

"An' all the lollipopses I can eat!"

Piero asked what lollipopses were. Angelica showed them the lollipops in her pocket. Piero agreed that the glassblower in town might be able to make something like that.

"An' fancy dresses! An' servants to wait on me like I was a princess, an' a throne to sit in, right here in my palace!"

Piero frowned. "But the Palazzo Vecchio belongs to the Republic," he said.

"It's my palace now," Angelica said.

Kimi rolled her eyes. "Oh, brother!"

The men muttered amongst themselves. Angelica tried to listen in.

"It is too much to ask . . ." one man protested.

"But if the wise one can help us . . ." another man said.

"Remember the signs . . . !" warned a third.

Finally, Machiavelli stepped forward. "*Signorina*, you know how to get what you want."

"So what'll you give me?" Angelica asked.

Machiavelli said quickly, "Anything you want! If only you will tell us how to get the money we need to protect Florence."

"Good!" Angelica reached into her pocket. "I gots the answer to your problem right here. All the money you need."

She poured change out of her pocket. It fell to the floor in a glittering stream. "Take 'em. I got lots more in my piggy bank at home."

The men looked on in wonder until one of them, a goldsmith, bit down on one of the coins. He threw it back to the floor in disgust. "These coins are but base metal!" He sneered. "Together they are worth less than just one of our own gold florins!"

The men glared at Angelica. They didn't seem very impressed with her anymore.

"It's not my fault! That's all you get for a boo-boo where I come from," Angelica said.

Piero sneered. "And where is that, *principessa?*"

Angelica didn't answer. She was too busy trying to figure out something that would make her look smart again. Then she thought of something. "Listen, I gots something wise to say," she announced.

Angelica's brow crinkled as she tried to remember some of the fancy language that Grandpa Lou thought was so great.

"Oh yeah," she said, smiling brightly at the council. "Say-la-grr."

The men drew back in surprise. "Did the wise one say, *'C'est la guerre'?*" one member asked. Matteo shook his head at Angelica, trying to get her to keep quiet, but she didn't notice.

"Yes," Angelica proudly replied, thinking that the man was impressed. She said it again for good measure, even more loudly this time. "SAY-LA-GRR!"

Piero's face turned purple.

"French! The wise one is a spy! She is plotting war!" Piero snarled, then cast an angry look at the babies.

"Uh-oh," said Chuckie. "I think we're in trouble."

CHAPTER 11

"Let's get out of here!" Chuckie said. The babies got ready to run. But the way out the door was blocked by the men.

"Seize them!" Piero commanded Matteo. The poor boy looked at his new friends in dismay and took a small step in their direction.

"And release the hounds!" Piero bellowed in Machiavelli's ear.

Machiavelli looked in confusion at the lapdog asleep in his arms. "But I have only one small puppy."

"Then release the puppy!" Piero shrieked.

Machiavelli shrugged and gently placed his little pug on the floor. "Attack!" he commanded, pointing at the babies. The puppy pranced over to Angelica, wagging its tail. It just wanted to play. But Angelica and the babies were still in trouble.

"Now what'll we do?" Chuckie moaned.

"How will we get out?" Kimi cried, looking around wildly.

"I said, seize them!" Piero gave Matteo a shove.

"Uh . . . look out! I am coming to get you now," Matteo told the babies loudly, winking at them. He had finally thought of a way to repay Angelica for dumping water on her head.

Matteo looked Angelica right in the eye. "You had better not climb out that window!"

That was all the hint Angelica needed. She scrambled up on her chair and jumped for the low, narrow window.

But just as Angelica was almost through, she got stuck again. The doll's big silk skirts were too fluffy to fit.

"Please, Angelica! Just drop the doll!" Chuckie yelled, waiting his turn.

But Angelica wouldn't let go of her treasure. She wiggled in the window like a worm in its hole.

Meanwhile, Piero was staring angrily at Matteo. "Are you a yellow-bellied coward or just a beetle-headed half-wit? Why do you tarry so?"

"Quickly now!" Matteo whispered to Angelica.

"I'm not leaving my doll!" Angelica replied. But at that moment the puppy jumped up and nipped at her dangling foot, thinking she was playing.

"Owwww!" Angelica swatted at the puppy. That made her drop the doll, and Angelica tumbled out the window, disappearing into the bushes below.

Chuckie and Kimi scrambled after her.

"After them! Make haste, you knock-kneed measle!" Piero shouted at Matteo. "We will take up the chase outside, once we have summoned the guard!"

An instant later Matteo tumbled out the window.

"We only have moments," he warned the babies. "Let us be off to the church."

But before they got very far, they heard Piero calling for the guards and the sounds of feet thundering through the palazzo.

"I know another way!" Matteo led Angelica and the babies along a side street to the church.

Once inside, they spotted Tommy sitting glumly on a fancy carved bench. Tied to his back with yards of skinny string were a pair of lopsided wings clumsily cut from a scrap of paper.

"Boy, am I glad to see you guys!" Tommy said, smiling.

The church had been cleared out to make space for Michelangelo to work. All the walls were covered with his sketches of heads, feet, and hands. A tall ladder leaned up against one side of the church, and the artist stood at the very top, moving some sketches tacked to the wall.

When Angelica banged the door shut behind the babies, Michelangelo swung around. That was a mistake.

The babies watched from the floor, frozen. "He's gonna fall!" Kimi yelled.

CHAPTER 12

Hearing the door slam, Michelangelo had turned around and was now teetering on the ladder, about ten feet above the floor. His arms spun like pinwheels. "Help!"

Then Tommy saw something that he thought would help. "Grab on to the swing!" he shouted to Michelangelo.

Tommy pointed up at a wooden platform that workers used to wash the tall windows inside the church. The platform hung by long ropes from the beams near the church balcony, not far from Michelangelo's ladder. It looked like a giant swing hanging there.

Michelangelo reached out for the platform. He grabbed on to the edge just as the ladder fell over with a tremendous CRASH!

"I cannot climb up!" Michelangelo hollered. The platform was swinging wildly, and Michelangelo couldn't pull himself up.

"We must make it steady or he will surely fall!" Matteo cried. He pointed at the ropes dangling from the platform. "Each of you, seize a rope!"

Angelica, Matteo, and the babies raced over to grab the ropes. They hung on, swinging back and forth an inch above the floor, trying to steady the platform for Michelangelo.

"It's not working, Tommy!" Kimi gasped.

Just then the church door banged open once again. There in the doorway stood Phil and Lil, with Dil! "We've been looking for you, Tommy," Phil said.

"We hearded you from outside," Lil said. She looked at the other babies swinging back and forth just above the floor, their toes scraping the thick dust that lay on the church floor.

"We wanna play too!" Lil said.

"Grab on!" Tommy yelled, swinging by like a pendulum.

The twins left Dil in his stroller and ran over. Each of them grabbed a rope.

"Wheeooo!" Dil crowed, clapping happily as he watched.

"It's working! Just . . . hang . . . on," Matteo gasped.

A minute later Michelangelo hoisted himself up. "Safe at last!" he cried, lying flat on his back along the narrow platform. He stared up at the ceiling, panting with relief.

Down below, the babies let go of the ropes.

"That was fun!" Lil said.

"Can we do it again?" Phil asked.

The other babies just groaned.

Suddenly Michelangelo's voice rang out. "What an idea! I am a genius!"

Everyone looked up to see him peering down over the edge of the platform, smiling widely. "I know how I shall paint the ceiling of the Sistine Chapel if the Pope calls me to Rome."

He pretended to swish a brush across an imaginary ceiling. "I shall use a platform like this one and paint like so. I will be much faster. Then I can return to my sculpting, eh?"

"But how are you gonna get down now?" Kimi asked.

Michelangelo's smile faded. "That is a problem."

Matteo, Angelica, and the babies tried lifting the ladder, but it was too heavy.

"You must go for help," Michelangelo told the babies.

"Uh-uh!" Angelica shook her head. "Not

while those meanies from the palace are out there, looking for us. I'm not going anywheres!"

Matteo explained about the council and the guards chasing them.

To make matters worse, at that moment Dil started crying again. Michelangelo groaned. "Is my situation not bad enough without the *bambino* wailing so? I am stuck here! I tell you, not even the great Leonardo da Vinci can help me escape from this nightmare!" Michelangelo sighed dramatically.

"Do not despair, Michelangelo. I will save you," a deep voice boomed from the depths of the balcony and seemed to echo throughout the church like a bell.

"Wh-who is that?" Chuckie wondered.

The other babies stared at the figure standing high above them on the balcony. The man had a very old face, lined with wrinkles. A white beard and mustache flowed from beneath his big, beaky nose.

"Take my hand," the man called to Michelangelo. He leaned out as far as he could and stretched a long arm toward Michelangelo. The angels carved into the wooden wall of the balcony seemed to hover behind his head.

Michelangelo sniffed. "I might have known you would make me look foolish," he complained. But Michelangelo sat up on the platform and reached one hand toward the old man. The next instant, Michelangelo was safely on the balcony. The babies heard the two men talking as they descended the stairs.

"And what brings you here in time for my rescue?" Michelangelo was saying in a snippy tone.

"I came only to see what you are doing for the palazzo," the old man replied. "I am finished with my own cartoon and hoped to see yours."

The two men appeared at the foot of the balcony steps. The old man walked slowly over to the group of babies and looked down at them with a grave face. But a twinkle lurked in his dark eyes. "*Buona sera*," he said in greeting.

"Ungee!" Dil sniffled.

The old man reached down and tickled Dil under the chin. "Coochi-coochi-coo," he said in his soothing voice. Dil stopped crying in an instant. He seemed entranced by the white beard, kind eyes, and deep voice.

"Okay, okay, who is that guy?" Angelica asked loudly.

Michelangelo rolled his eyes. "*Who?* He is the one you seek! It is Leonardo da Vinci himself!"

CHAPTER 13

"You see, *bambini,* I am not so special," da Vinci said for the umpteenth time. He tapped his white-haired head. "Just an ordinary brain after all."

Michelangelo snorted. "Do not be so modest, Leonardo. You know that everyone in Florence—all of Italy—thinks you are a genius."

Da Vinci shook his head and sighed.

"You rescued Milk-and-angel," Phil said.

"An' you made Dil stop crying just by lookin' at him," Lil added.

"You've just gots to help us, too,"

Tommy said. "See, we gots a—"

But before Tommy could tell da Vinci about Dactar, the great master said, "I am afraid I am of no use or help to anyone these days. Once, perhaps, the world thought me clever, but no more."

Da Vinci turned to Michelangelo. "It is the young ones like yourself the patrons will turn to now."

"Bah!" Michelangelo spat.

The old man shook his head. "I always must be thinking of some new invention, some new philosophy, some new way to paint, or I will be forgotten."

"Hear that, Tommy?" Angelica said. "He's not gonna help anyone."

Suddenly Angelica wanted to go home. She was tired of running away from the guards and she missed Cynthia. Home was also where her parents treated her like a real princess.

"The deal's off!" Angelica snapped at

Michelangelo. "We found da Binky, and I didn't get to play with my doll, so Tommy doesn't have to be your angel anymore and we can go now."

"Well, I am finished, anyway!" Michelangelo retorted. He tacked a drawing up on the wall and stepped aside to show off his creation. It was an angel, all right, only it didn't look much like Tommy, except for the diaper and the wings. "This angel will become a bit of my ceiling for the Pope, you will see. It will serve as the model for all my little angels," Michelangelo said.

Then a new thought seemed to strike the artist, and he began another sketch. "I am done with you now, *bambino*," he said absently as he drew.

"C'mon you guys, help me out of these wingie-things," Tommy said. He couldn't wait to take them off. The other babies toddled over to help.

Meanwhile, Michelangelo was working

intently, and a second beautiful picture was taking shape. "Yes! Yes, I see it now. I will put two figures on the ceiling of the chapel, two great men who reach to one another across a blue sky."

"Maybe that will be your Mister Peas," Kimi said.

Michelangelo crowed softly to himself. "Yes, it will be a masterpiece! Michelangelo is a genius!"

Da Vinci stepped over for a closer look and nodded slowly. "You are indeed a great artist! People are foolish to call you merely a sculptor."

"WHAT?" Michelangelo threw down his chalk. "Merely a sculptor?" he shouted. "Why, that is the most noble of all the arts. Painting and drawing pretty pictures—bah!"

In a temper, he pulled the drawing off the wall. It looked like he was about to rip it to pieces.

"No!" Tommy cried. "Please don't rip it!"

"It's too prettyful!" Lil added.

Michelangelo stopped just as he was about to tear the picture to shreds. The small faces looking so worried made his rage disappear. He smoothed out his picture and broke out in a grin. "It is good, no?" he boasted.

Then Michelangelo flapped his hands impatiently at the babies. "I must get busy. I have a new cartoon to make. So be off with you!"

He flung open the door. With a last nudge from Michelangelo, the others all found themselves standing outside in the piazza. "*Arrivederci!*" Michelangelo said shortly, just before slamming the door in the faces of the old man, Matteo, Angelica, and the babies.

"Wah!" Dil sounded like a police siren. "Waaaaah!"

Da Vinci looked down at the babies. What was he to do with them now?

CHAPTER 14

A guard posted in front of the palazzo heard Dil's cries and looked suspiciously across the piazza in their direction. Angelica tugged on the bottom of da Vinci's cloak.

"You better take us to your house," she warned him. "Or Matteo's master is gonna throw us all in a dumbgeon. You too, I bet."

"What do you mean—?" da Vinci began to ask, looking puzzled.

But Tommy interrupted by tugging on the artist's cloak. "No, first you gots to fix—"

But at that instant, the guard cried a warning. "The French spies! They are here!"

Da Vinci frowned. "Is he mad? Anyone with half a wit can see you are no spies."

"My master has no wits at all when his anger boils!" Matteo cried. "I tell you, sir, we must flee!"

The old man nodded and headed off down a narrow alley. "I will help you. This way!"

"Hurry up, slowpokes!" Angelica shouted to the babies. She kept looking over her shoulder to see if anyone was following them. Just as they turned the corner, Angelica spotted a crowd racing into the piazza. "Faster!" she cried, then heaved a sigh of relief when she saw the mob head the other way.

"My studio is just over the *ponte*," da Vinci told the children, pointing to a flat stone bridge up ahead of them. "Once across the river, we will be safe."

Once inside the artist's cluttered work space, Dil reminded everyone he was hungry again with a howl. Da Vinci quickly handed around bowls of goat's milk with thick slabs of bread soaking inside.

"Yuck," Angelica said, wrinkling her nose in disgust. She popped a lollipop in her mouth instead and began to wander around da Vinci's studio.

"I like it," Lil said, guzzling the last drop from her bowl.

"Me too," Phil agreed.

Tommy was so hungry, he didn't care what it tasted like. "It's not so bad. An' it made Dil stop crying."

Da Vinci looked at the empty bowls. "Poor, hungry *bambini!* Perhaps I have some grapes left still on the arbor outside," he said as he headed out to the garden.

Just then Angelica spotted something interesting. "Hmm . . . what have we here?" she muttered. She was looking at a painting in the corner, sitting all by itself on an easel lit by the glow from the only window in the room.

The babies gathered around for a closer look.

Lil gasped. "Oooh! That lady doesn't gots a face!"

Chuckie covered his face with his hands. It was true. The lady in the portrait had long dark hair parted in the middle and sat with hands folded delicately on her lap—but she had no face. There was just blank white canvas where her eyes, nose, and mouth should be. It was pretty spooky. Even the background was filled with mysterious shapes.

"It's not scary," Angelica snorted.

"Oh, yeah?" Kimi looked Angelica right in the eye. "If you're not a-scared, why are you standin' way over there?"

"Am not!" Angelica stuck out her

tongue at Kimi and stepped closer to the painting. She brushed her hand over a corner of the painting. "See?"

"Look what you did, Angelica!" Chuckie cried. "You made it all goopy!"

Angelica gasped. The painting was still a little wet, and a corner of the background was now smeared.

"Now da Binky's really not gonna help us fix Dactar," said Phil.

Matteo looked nervously at the door. "Perhaps it can be fixed before he returns," he suggested.

Angelica tried to rub the smear away, but that just made it worse. Now that whole corner was blurry.

"Maybe he won't notice," Kimi said nervously.

But it was too late. "WHAT HAVE YOU DONE?" da Vinci shouted. He stood in the doorway staring at his painting in horror.

CHAPTER 15

The babies froze. Da Vinci's face now looked like it was carved from stone.

"I didn't do nuthin'!" Angelica said, backing away from the painting. She looked around wildly, then pointed a finger at Dil. "He did it!"

"Yucky!" Dil burbled.

But everyone could see that Angelica's hand was covered with paint. Da Vinci stomped across the studio. "You have destroyed my work!" da Vinci stormed. "It is ruined! It is . . ."

He snatched the canvas off its easel to look at it more closely. "Very interesting!"

he finished in a totally different tone of voice. The old man brought the painting so close to his face, his nose almost touched the canvas. "Yes, most intriguing!"

Da Vinci turned to the babies, a gleam in his eyes. "For a long time I try different styles of painting, like this," he said, pointing to the painting. "You see her hands, the way there are no lines? I use only light and shadow to show one finger here, another there."

The babies nodded. They could see that her hands were very nice.

"I am the master of this, people say. But still, I look for something else that is new," he added. "Something to make those who look at the portrait *feel* the painting, not only see it!"

Angelica was definitely feeling very relieved that da Vinci was not mad at her.

Da Vinci beamed at Angelica. "Now, little one, you have found the answer!"

He pointed at the blurry corner. "You have made it seem that we look at the landscape through a haze . . . through smoke."

The babies saw the corner Angelica had smudged.

"It inspires me to a new way of painting," da Vinci said. "I will show the shapes not with line or shadows, but with a blur of color." He beamed at Angelica. "*Grazie, signorina!*"

Angelica was just about to tell him how he could pay her back, when a soft voice called out. "*Signore?*"

The babies looked up. There in the doorway stood a lady with long, dark hair, parted in the middle.

"*Signore* Leonardo," she said, "is it not time for me to pose for my portrait?"

Everyone recognized the woman. It was the scary lady from the painting!

CHAPTER 16

The babies were relieved to see that the real lady had a face, though. Da Vinci hurried over and motioned the woman to a seat in the corner. "If you will sit down, I will be with you in one moment."

Da Vinci looked down at the babies and scratched his head. "I must work now, little ones. You will play here quietly, please, while the lady sits for her portrait. Later we will decide what is to be done with you."

He turned to Matteo. "Perhaps you will help, young sir?" da Vinci asked. The boy eagerly sprang to the artist's side. He filled his arms with paint pots and brushes.

While da Vinci and Matteo moved off to the corner, Phil, Lil, Chuckie, and Kimi found a crate filled with sticks of chalk. Within moments, they were all busy coloring.

Kimi picked up a piece of chalk and started drawing mustaches on some of da Vinci's sketches of heads. Dil watched her and clapped in delight.

"Hey, guys, we can't play now," Tommy reminded the other babies. "We gots to fix Dactar, 'member?"

Angelica laughed. "Oh, yeah? You're just a bunch a' dumb babies! If da Binky can't help us fix Dactar, then he's broked for good. An' we'll never get home."

Suddenly all the babies stopped what they were doing. Angelica was right—they needed Dactar to get back home!

"Tommy! She's wrong, right?" Chuckie asked hopefully.

"A'course she is, Chuckie," Kimi said, but she wasn't so sure.

"We wanna go home!" Phil and Lil said together. They began to sniffle.

Even Angelica felt funny. She'd just been teasing Tommy, but now that she thought about it, she wanted to go home too!

"Don't worry, guys," Tommy said. "I'll think of something."

Just then da Vinci walked over to get some chalk. He blinked at the sight of their worried faces. "What is wrong now, *bambini?*" he asked.

Tommy blurted out, "See, we gots this flying machine that's broked and—"

The artist stared at Tommy in amazement. A spark lit his dark eyes like a flame. "*Scusa!* But did you say you have a flying machine?" he asked excitedly.

CHAPTER 17

"It is true, then? You have flown in this machine?" Da Vinci was staring in wonder at Stu's diagram of the Dactar flying machine. Tommy had fished Stu's diagram out of his diaper, and now da Vinci was looking at it as if it were a precious piece of art.

"Always, I have said that humankind can achieve anything, including flight," he said. "But the world only laughs."

He slapped the paper. "But now you say there is a working model of this machine. That would prove to the world that man can do anything he dreams! It is a work of genius!"

Tommy puffed up with pride. He'd always known his daddy was smart. But here was a genuine genius who thought the same thing.

"If Uncle Stu's so smart how come Dactar got broked?" Angelica said.

"The flying machine is broken?" da Vinci asked.

Angelica sighed. "Yeah, it fell down, and one part rolled away into the water. Plus a wing is all bent."

"What did the lost part look like?" da Vinci asked.

"Like a big plate but with pointy teeth all around," Kimi remembered.

Da Vinci grabbed a charcoal and paper and began sketching.

When he was done, he showed his drawing to Angelica, Matteo, and the babies. "Like this?" he asked eagerly.

The babies all nodded their heads. "A little," Angelica said.

"Hmm . . . so it only misses a gear . . ." da Vinci looked up with a broad smile. "*Bambini*, I think I can help you."

The babies' eyes grew wide with hope. "You can?" Tommy asked. Maybe da Binky could save them after all.

Da Vinci nodded. "I invented a gear of a special kind much like this. It was used in my own designs for flying machines, so perhaps it will work in yours."

"Forget the stupid ear. If you've got a flying machine, why don't we just use that?" Angelica demanded.

Da Vinci looked disheartened. "My machines were never built." He waved a hand over the mess of papers on the floor, covered with drawings of machines, ship's hulls, dams, and fancy buildings.

"How come?" Chuckie wanted to know.

Da Vinci smiled sadly. "When I am in the middle of an idea—poof!—soon another comes to take its place." He tapped his skull. "My brain is full of such things. Too many to chase just one idea, I think."

"Okay, okay," Angelica said impatiently. "Let's just—"

But da Vinci interrupted as his face brightened. "I did not build my machines, but perhaps the gear designed long ago can be made to work in your own machine. The sketch is somewhere"—he looked around the room—"and we must find it!"

The babies looked in dismay at the collection of thousands of papers. All were covered in scribbled drawings and notes.

Suddenly the lady called out, "*Signore* Leonardo!"

"You see it is true what I say. Poof! I have forgotten the poor *signora*." The artist threw up his hands. "I am eager to fix your machine, but I must finish the portrait first. You must find the sketch without me, then we will see about your machine!" He and Matteo hurried back to the lady and her portrait.

"We'll never find the picture!" Chuckie said, looking around at the sloppy stacks of notebooks, papers, and drawings.

"Sure we will, Chuckie," Tommy reassured his friend. "We'll all look, even Dil."

Dil gurgled and upset a pile of papers that slid across the floor like lava, making even more of a mess.

Soon the babies were diaper-deep in drawings. They found pictures of canals, magnificent buildings, faces, and figures. There were drawings of birds and horses, feet and hands.

"Lookit this one," Phil said. The babies stared at a drawing of a man turning a cartwheel inside a big circle. They found drawings of flying machines, tanks, ships, and parachutes, but no gear. After a while, Angelica got tired of looking and wandered over to da Vinci, who was staring glumly at his painting.

"Is the pose not good?" the lady asked nervously.

"Yes, it is good, *signora*," da Vinci said. "But perhaps if you look over to the left? Like so."

The lady looked over to the left. She was just in time to see Kimi draw a red mustache on da Vinci's picture of the man in the wheel. The lady's lips twitched, but then she looked serious again.

Da Vinci lifted his chalk to the white space on the portrait, but did not make a mark. His hand fell to his side and he groaned. "I cannot paint her face even after so many months."

"Why not?" asked Angelica. "You're supposed to be a great painter."

"Because I wish to create something new!" he exclaimed. "And the only way to make a portrait that is truly new each time you see it is to capture something in the face that can be found nowhere else."

"Like what?" Angelica wanted to know. Matteo leaned forward eagerly to hear too.

"I must have a smile that has never been seen before," Da Vinci said. "I work for a year, but still I do not find one. And the lady refuses to smile because it is the custom now to be stern for portraits."

Da Vinci clearly wasn't looking at the lady's face just then, because she didn't look stern at all. Her eyes were lit with laughter at the sight of the babies struggling to reach the top of a tall pile of notebooks.

"Look out!" Tommy shouted as the pile started to topple. The other babies hurried out of the way as the notebooks fell over with a thud.

One sheet fluttered down and landed near the lady. She stared at it out of the corner of her eye. Suddenly, a small, secret smile escaped.

Da Vinci looked up then and caught the tiny grin. "*La!* There!" He stared at the lady, entranced. "That is the smile I have searched for!"

The babies turned to the lady, whose smile was frozen on her face. Da Vinci stared a moment longer, then he snatched up a piece of charcoal and leaped to his easel.

In a moment, a face began to take shape in the empty space in the middle.

"The mouth—just so!" da Vinci was muttering to himself. "The line of the eyes—precisely." Da Vinci sketched with rapid strokes of his charcoal. Soon his fingers were blackened, and a smear appeared on his nose.

Da Vinci finally stepped away from the easel. The babies crowded close for a look.

"It's nice," Chuckie nodded.

Da Vinci was glowing with happiness. "You have given me my smile!" he told the babies. "*Grazie, bambini!* How may I ever repay you?"

"Fix Dactar!" Tommy said quickly.

"If I only had my old notes," the artist said, shaking his head.

"*Signore* Leonardo?" the lady said, holding up the sheet of notepaper that had fallen beside her. "Is this what you and the *bambini* seek?" she asked.

It was a sheet with fancy, spidery writing all along the sides of the picture, which showed a complex-looking gear.

"*Signora!*" Da Vinci grabbed the sheet and kissed the lady's hand until she blushed. "You are indeed a masterpiece!"

The babies held their breath as da Vinci compared his drawing with Stu's diagram of Dactar. "Yes, yes, I believe it just might succeed," the old man mumbled. "But I must read my notes to see precisely the size and shape and angle of the teeth."

Da Vinci took the paper over to a large speckled mirror that hung on one wall and held the sheet up to the glass.

"Why are you doing that?" Kimi asked curiously.

Da Vinci laughed. "It is a little trick of mine. I write the notes for my inventions backward, you see? So I must use a mirror to read it the right way."

"Is it a way to keep your inventions secret?" Matteo asked.

"That is what my rivals believe. They think my notes conceal something precious or perhaps dangerous," da Vinci said. Then he waggled the fingers of one hand. "Truly, it is because I work with the left hand. The ink, it smears when I write forward."

Just then Angelica interrupted with a loud, "Shhhh! Listen!"

"Search every inch of every home!" came the sound of a voice shouting in the distance.

Matteo turned pale. "It is my master! We have no time to lose," he warned da Vinci.

The artist threw up his hands. "Yes, we have to hurry. But first the gear must be made. And I am no worker of stone, wood, or metal," he told them. "For this we need a blacksmith or a builder."

"What about a sculptor?" the lady ventured.

And the babies cried out, "Milk-and-angel!"

CHAPTER 18

Knock. Knock.

"Go away!" Michelangelo shouted from behind the wooden door of the church.

Knock. Knock. Knock.

Da Vinci rapped on the door again. This time Michelangelo didn't even bother to answer.

"What'll we do now?" Tommy gulped.

"Stop being so nice about it," Angelica said, shoving da Vinci aside. She pounded on the door with her hands and feet. BANG! BANG-BANG! BANG! BANG! "Lemme in!" Angelica screeched.

The door was thrown open. Angelica's

foot was already poised for a kick, so she ended up giving Michelangelo's shin a good whack.

"Owwww!" he wailed, hopping on one foot.

"Don't be a baby," Angelica snapped, marching past him into the church. "If you'd opened the door before, I wouldn't have kicked you!"

"I told you to go away," Michelangelo growled, nursing his bruised shin. He was surprised to see such a crowd. There were the babies, Angelica, Matteo, da Vinci, and a lady Michelangelo had never seen before.

"Why do you come here?" He snarled at them all.

Da Vinci told him.

But Michelangelo wasn't in the mood to help anyone. "I am too busy!" he said. "I must draw night and day, so that when the Pope calls me, I can surprise him with the work I have already done." Michelangelo rubbed his hands together gleefully.

"No, my friend," da Vinci said, shaking his head. "You must first aid the *bambini*."

Michelangelo flew into a rage and stomped around the church shouting angrily at the walls. "It is a waste of my talents as a sculptor! I refuse!" he stormed.

Everyone fell silent. "You gotta help us," Tommy finally said. "We saved your life, 'member?"

"It is a matter of honor, *signore*," Matteo added. "Remember that they aided you when you were in trouble."

"I was only in trouble because of them," Michelangelo sulked. But he knew Matteo was right. The artist sighed dramatically. "Very well. Show me the plans!"

The babies waited breathlessly while he looked over Stu's diagram and da

Vinci's sketch. Then Michelangelo looked up. "It can be done, old man," he said. "But only because I, too, am a genius!"

The babies grinned and hugged each other. They were going home!

Michelangelo found tools and some scraps of metal he used for building frames for plaster molds. He explained that he tried out poses for his statues using the molds, before making them in stone. "This is strong enough, I think," he muttered, inspecting a small sheet of metal.

Michelangelo wasted no time. Soon the gear was done, and he blew the last bit of metal dust away. "A fine piece of work," he said with pride.

Da Vinci nodded. "Yes, it is a good job of carving . . . for a painter."

"I am a SCULPTOR!" Michelangelo roared, before he realized da Vinci was teasing.

Matteo helped gather up the tools that

were needed to fix Dactar. The lady offered to push Dil in his stroller. Then the artists led the babies and their new friends out of the church.

"Quickly now!" Da Vinci pointed toward a narrow stone lane. "We must use streets too small to hold the mob," he explained in a whisper.

The babies nodded. They could hear the noise of shouting not too far away. It was all the warning they needed to keep quiet. Even Angelica kept her mouth shut as they followed the two artists through back alleys and byways.

When they reached the town gate, Matteo tugged at da Vinci's cloak.

"The guards will have been told to watch for us," he said in a worried voice. "I fear they will stop any children who try to pass."

Everyone looked discouraged. Then Chuckie's voice piped up. "I gots an idea."

The babies looked around, but didn't

see their friend. Then Chuckie's head popped out from under the folds of Michelangelo's cloak. "No one will see us in here. It's like playing hide-an'-seek behind the curtains."

Tommy smiled. "Great idea, Chuckie!"

The lady held Dil her arms under her cloak. Michelangelo put the tools in the stroller so it would look more like a fancy wheelbarrow. Angelica, Matteo, and the babies quickly gathered under the grown-ups' cloaks.

Minutes later da Vinci, Michelangelo, and the lady strolled past the guards. The watchmen, delighted at catching a glimpse of the famous artisans, didn't even notice that their long cloaks and her wide skirt looked a little lumpy.

Once out of sight past the gates, the children peeked out. "Uncle Stu's crummy 'vention is right up there!" Angelica pointed toward the hill. It wasn't long before the group reached Dactar's crash site.

Da Vinci examined the flying machine with stunned joy. Michelangelo tsked-tsked over the broken wing, but had no problem repairing it with his tools. Then he installed the gear while da Vinci directed him.

"The bird, he is ready to fly now!" da Vinci said at last.

"You fixed my daddy's flying machine!" Tommy cheered.

The happy scene was interrupted by a loud yell. "There they are, the scoundrels. And my scurvy runner among them!"

It was Piero. He stood at the bottom of the hill shaking his fist.

At the sight of his master, Matteo hid behind da Vinci. Michelangelo shook his own fist at Piero. Then the artist turned to Matteo, and his frown melted. "I promise you will have nothing to fear from this day's work, young man," he said. "Piero

Soderini cannot stand up against the great Michelangelo!"

Da Vinci agreed. "A well-spent day brings worthy sleep," he told Matteo. "Know this—I will take you on as my apprentice. You will never have to return to your master's house again."

The lady hugged Matteo close as the boy smiled happily.

Then da Vinci turned to the babies and told them to hurry. "You are outsiders, so I fear even our stature cannot spare you a visit to a Florentine dungeon," he warned them. He cast a worried glance at Piero and his guards, who were getting closer every moment. "It is time you were off."

The babies rushed to hug their friends. "Thank you! Thank you!"

Tommy smiled up at Matteo. "'Specially you, Matteo."

Chuckie nodded. "You saveded us from those scary guys."

Matteo grinned and swept into a low bow. "I was pleased to be of service, *bambini*. It was truly an honor."

"Serving Princess Angelica is better than working for that dumb council," Angelica agreed. "Now, let's get outta here before they throw us in the dumbgeon."

Angelica scrambled into the flying machine first. Then the artists, Matteo, and the lady lifted the babies into the cockpit.

The minute da Vinci strapped Dil into his baby seat, Tommy's brother reached for the big red button. The artist barely had time to jump out of the way as smoke began to spew out of the flying machine. "Now, the world shall see that humankind can fly!" da Vinci cried out with joy.

Da Vinci stared in awe as Dactar finally lifted off the ground and rose high into the air. The machine made a lazy circle in the sky and began to fly away.

Below them, Piero had finally reached the top of the hill. He hopped about, howling with rage. But the guards and townspeople looked up in amazement and waved cheerfully at the babies in their flying machine.

Safe inside Dactar, the babies waved back. "At least now there are lots of people to see that da Binky was right," Tommy said. "They'll see Dactar fly an' know da Binky was smart after all."

He joined Angelica and the other babies in calling good-bye as everyone below grew smaller and smaller.

"Good-bye!"

"*Arrivederci!*"

CHAPTER 19

The breeze was gentle, and the flying machine rocked like a cradle in the air. The babies' eyes slid shut as they listened to the gentle tones from the CD.

"*Dov'è il bagno?* Where is the bathroom? *Buona notte.* Good night."

Tommy blinked sleepily. He saw they were passing through a cloud. The cloud thinned just as his eyes opened again, and Tommy gasped. "Hey, look!" He nudged Kimi, who was dozing beside him. "We're back!"

Sure enough, they were sitting in Tommy's backyard. The only cloud around them now was the smoke that belched from Dactar's engine.

Just then the door to the house flew open.

"Lou, I thought you were watching the kids!" Didi yelled as the grown-ups tumbled out in a rush.

Grandpa Lou held up a mop. "How'd I know it would take so long to find this pesky thing?"

"No harm done, Deed," Stu added. "The kids are safe and sound in their playpen—"

At that instant, the Dactar flying machine belched another puff of smoke with a rude PFFFTTTT. The grown-ups looked over in surprise.

"Where'd all that smoke come from?" Stu asked, waving it away with his hands. "I guess the exhaust fan blew."

"The babies!" Didi gasped. "They're in Dactar!"

The grown-ups hurried over to the flying machine.

"How in tarnation did you sprouts get in there?" Grandpa Lou wondered as he carried Phil and Lil over to the playpen.

"They must have crawled over," Lulu said. She smiled down at Kimi in her arms.

"My goodness." Didi smiled as she lifted Dil out of Dactar. "You babies crawled in here by yourselves? You must've had fun!"

"You don't know the half of it," Angelica muttered.

Stu settled Tommy and Chuckie in the playpen. "Looks like you wanted to go for a ride, didn't you? Good thing you babies couldn't reach any of the buttons in there."

Lulu nodded. "Goodness, no! We wouldn't want any babies flying around."

The grown-ups laughed at the thought.

"I wish I could get Dactar to fly," Stu said. He opened the hood of the engine for another look. Then he leaned closer. "Funny, I hadn't realized what a great design this is," he said, tapping one of the gears with his screwdriver. "This gear here looks a little like something I remember from da Vinci's sketches. I guess I was influenced by the great man himself when I built it."

He looked at Didi smugly. "You know, Deed," he said, "I'm beginning to think I'm a regular Renaissance man myself."

Tommy looked around at his friend and whispered. "Only my daddy is even smarter than da Binky."

Angelica snorted.

"He is!" Lil agreed. "Da Binky didn't even make his 'ventions, but Tommy's daddy builds 'em all the time."

"Only none of them work," Angelica pointed out.

"Some of 'em work . . . kind of!" Kimi retorted. "Dactar flew all the way to Little-ee," she reminded Angelica.

Angelica couldn't argue with that. But

she still could complain. "I don't care who's smart and who's not," she growled loudly. "I still didn't get my fancy doll!"

Didi overheard Angelica's remark. "Oh, that reminds me!" She rushed back into the house.

A minute later Didi came out with Cynthia. Angelica gasped when she saw the doll's outfit, which was a fancy long gown covered with sparkly jewels. "Cynthia, you're beautiful!" she cried.

Didi smiled. "When I was a little girl, my mother made this dress for my own doll. After you left Cynthia here yesterday, it reminded me that I still had the dress upstairs."

"Now Cynthia looks just like a princess," Angelica sighed. "A real princess—a *principessa*—just like me!"

Angelica rushed over to the playpen. "Look, babies!" she said as she showed off Cynthia's new dress.

"It's pretty, Angelica," said Kimi.

Chuckie smiled at Tommy. "That was a pretty good 'venture, huh, Tommy? 'Cept the part where that mean man was chasing us."

"I don't know what he was so upset about, anyways," Angelica said, shrugging. "I gave him all my pennies an' stuff. He shoulda treated a princess better."

Tommy smiled at his friends. "Yeah, but I'm sure glad we met da Binky."

THE END

About the Author

Maria Rosado has written many books and magazine articles for children. She studied journalism at the School of Visual Arts in New York City, where she also took drawing classes. Even though she never became as good an artist as Leonardo da Vinci, Maria can make complicated doodles in the margins of her notebook, and has added many good-looking mustaches to magazine pictures of people. Unlike Leonardo, she doesn't write backward because she uses a computer to type her stories. Maria just moved to Brooklyn, New York, with her husband and cat, and thinks that the hardest part about moving is remembering her new zip code!